HANDY HEALTH GUIDE
TO DIABETES

HANDY HEALTH GUIDES

Alvin and Virginia Silverstein
and Laura Silverstein Nunn

E **Enslow Publishers, Inc.**
40 Industrial Road
Box 398
Berkeley Heights, NJ 07922
USA
http://www.enslow.com

Original edition published as *Diabetes* in 2002.

Library of Congress Cataloging-in-Publication Data

Silverstein, Alvin.
Handy health guide to diabetes / by Alvin Silverstein, Virginia Silverstein, and Laura Silverstein Nunn.
pages cm. — (Handy health guides)
 Summary: "Find out what diabetes is, the different kinds of diabetes, diabetes testing, and how to treat it"— Provided
by publisher.
Includes bibliographical references and index.
 ISBN 978-0-7660-4275-9
 1. Diabetes—Juvenile literature. I. Silverstein, Virginia B. II. Nunn, Laura Silverstein. III. Title.
 RC660.S55 2014
 616.4'62—dc23
                              2012041452
Future editions:
Paperback ISBN: 978-1-4644-0493-1
EPUB ISBN: 978-1-4645-1255-1
Single-User PDF ISBN: 978-1-4646-1255-8
Multi-User PDF ISBN: 978-0-7660-5887-3

Printed in the United States of America

052013 Lake Book Manufacturing, Inc., Melrose Park, IL

10 9 8 7 6 5 4 3 2 1

To Our Readers: We have done our best to make sure all Internet Addresses in this book were active and appropriate
when we went to press. However, the author and the publisher have no control over and assume no liability for the
material available on those Internet sites or on other Web sites they may link to. Any comments or suggestions can be
sent by e-mail to comments@enslow.com or to the address on the back cover.

♻ Enslow Publishers, Inc., is committed to printing our books on recycled paper. The paper in every book contains
10% to 30% post-consumer waste (PCW). The cover board on the outside of each book contains 100% PCW. Our
goal is to do our part to help young people and the environment too!

Illustration Credits: © 2012 Clipart.com, pp. 9, 26 (left); CDC/Amanda Mills, p. 38; Comstock Images/
Photos.com, p. 4; DFree/Shutterstock.com, p. 21; Gayner Hallam/Photos.com, p. 40 (left); George Doyle/Photos.
com, p. 33; Igor Zakowski/Photos.com, p. 24; JDRF Walk to Cure Diabetes, Mike Young 2012, p. 37; Juergen Berger/
Science Source, p. 20; Keith Brofsky/Photos.com, p. 23; © Michael Newman/PhotoEdit, p. 42; Murat Erhan Okcu/
Photos.com, p. 27; Shutterstock.com, pp. 3, 6, 10, 12, 14, 15, 17, 18, 26 (right), 28, 29, 30, 40 (right).

Cover Photo: Shutterstock.com (all images)

CONTENTS

Some people are not able to use the sugar in food properly. They have diabetes.

1

THE SUGAR DISEASE

Most kids love to eat sweets. Ice cream, candy, and cake can make a day special, and a sweet dessert after dinner would be a nice treat. Sweet foods usually contain sugar—that's why they taste so good. But eating too many sweets isn't good for anybody. They can rot your teeth and keep you from eating foods that make you healthy and strong.

For some people, foods that contain sugar are not just unhealthy—they can be dangerous. Normally, your body turns sugar into energy you can use to do everyday activities—play, run, and even think. But some people are not able to use the sugar in their blood properly. They have a condition called diabetes. If you have diabetes, sometimes you might feel tired and confused. You might even faint or have to go to the hospital.

Regular exercise will help keep your body healthy.

Sweet Tooth

Do you have a sweet tooth? If you do, don't worry—you can't get diabetes from eating too many sweets. However, eating too much of that stuff can make you gain weight, which may lead to diabetes.

There is no cure for diabetes, but there are ways to keep the condition under control. Medications can prevent the symptoms. People often take a drug that must be injected into the skin. Exercising regularly and eating healthy foods are also important. With a good daily routine, a person with diabetes can live a long, healthy life.

2
WHAT IS DIABETES?

Diabetes is a disease in which the body cannot use sugar properly, and extra sugar builds up in the blood. Everybody has some sugar in their blood. It supplies the body with energy. But too much sugar in the blood can make you sick.

Normally, much of the food you eat is turned into a sugar called glucose. Some of the glucose is stored, and some of it is used directly for energy. Special chemicals, called hormones, are needed for the body to get the energy from sugar. These hormones are produced in the pancreas, an organ near your stomach.

Scattered throughout the pancreas are small blobs of tissue, called islets. Cells in the islets produce two important hormones, insulin and glucagon. These

What Is Sugar?

You probably think of sugar as that white stuff you sprinkle over your cereal or see people put in their coffee or tea. But that is only one kind of sugar. Sugars are found in sweet-tasting foods, such as fruits, candy, and ice cream. They belong to a food group called carbohydrates, which are the body's main source of energy. Another type of carbohydrate is starch. Starch is made up of a lot of sugar units linked together. Starchy foods include breads, pasta, and rice.

hormones are produced all the time, but the amounts sent out, or secreted, from the pancreas depend on how much sugar is already in the blood.

Both hormones work to control the body's use of sugar, but they have opposite effects on the blood. How do insulin and glucagon work?

After you eat, food is digested, or broken down, in your mouth, stomach, and intestines. The digestion process changes starches into sugars. Sugars and other food materials pass into your blood, which carries them to all parts of the body. Now it is time for insulin to go into action.

9

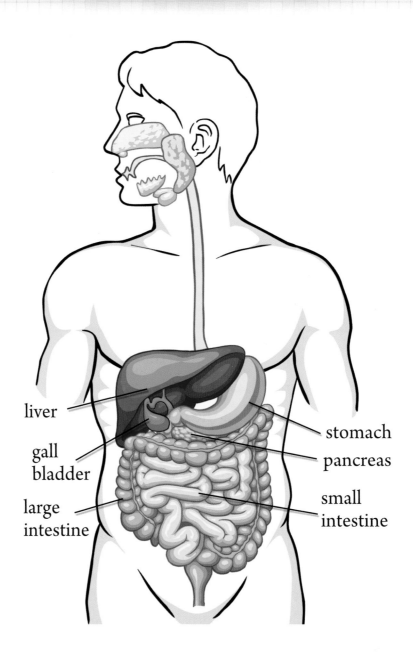

liver

gall
bladder

large
intestine

stomach

pancreas

small
intestine

Food passes from the mouth into the stomach and then on to the
intestines to be broken down by digestive juices from the pancreas.

Double-Duty

The pancreas is a double-duty organ. In addition to secreting the hormones insulin and glucagon from its islets, it also makes digestive juices. These juices help break down food so that your body can use it.

When the amount of glucose in the blood (the blood sugar level) rises, the pancreas secretes insulin. Insulin lowers the blood sugar level by helping glucose pass out of the blood and into the cells of the body. Some of the sugar in the body cells is used right away to produce energy. Some is changed into starch and fats and stored in the body. Starches and fats are handy forms to store sugar until the body needs some extra energy.

When the blood sugar level falls, the pancreas secretes more glucagon. This hormone makes the blood sugar level go up by causing starch in the cells to turn back into glucose. The glucose goes into the blood and is then carried to the cells that need energy.

Insulin and glucagon work together like members of a team. They make sure that the amount of sugar in the blood is always just right.

When the body cannot make enough insulin or cannot use the insulin properly, glucose cannot get into the cells. Eventually, extra sugar builds up in the blood, causing the symptoms of diabetes.

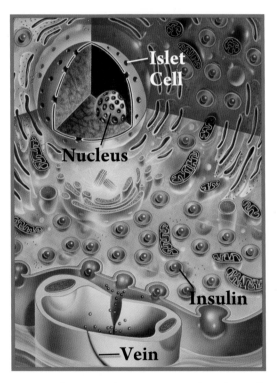

This diagram shows the organs in the digestive system, including the pancreas.

3

TYPES OF DIABETES

There are two main types of diabetes: type 1 and type 2. Both types result in too much sugar in the blood and produce similar symptoms. But there are some very important differences between the two.

Type 1 diabetes used to be called juvenile diabetes because it affects mainly children, teens, and young adults, but it can occur at any age. In type 1 diabetes, the pancreas no longer produces insulin. This can be very dangerous. Type 1 diabetes can appear suddenly. You may feel fine one day and then very sick the next. It is very important to correct the blood sugar level quickly to prevent life-threatening complications.

Type 2 diabetes is the most common form—it accounts for about 90 to 95 percent of all diabetes cases.

Type 1 diabetes affects mainly children and teenagers.

It affects mostly adults over age forty, although children may also develop this type of diabetes. In fact, doctors are seeing type 2 diabetes in an increasing number of young people these days, especially teenagers. In type 2 diabetes, the pancreas does produce insulin. However, it does not produce enough of it, or the body cannot use it properly. As a result, the body cells cannot get energy from sugar. Doctors call this condition insulin resistance. This type of diabetes can take years to develop.

In both types of diabetes, the body cells become starved for energy, and symptoms develop. Here are some warning signs of either type of diabetes.

You may:

- be thirsty all the time
- have to urinate frequently
- feel weak and tired
- feel hungry all the time
- lose weight, even though you eat a lot
- get sores on your skin that take a long time to heal
- notice that objects look fuzzy or blurry
- have pains in your legs

Anybody can have some of these warning signs from time to time without having diabetes. But if you have many of these signs, and have them all the time, you should see a doctor.

People with diabetes have sugar in their urine. How does sugar get in

One sign of diabetes is being thirsty all the time.

the urine? Urine is made in the kidneys. The kidneys remove waste products from the blood. They also take out some water, to flush the wastes away. If there is too much of something in the blood, the kidneys take that out, too. For people with diabetes there is too much sugar in their blood, and soon sugar turns up in their urine.

When sugar passes into the urine, the urine gets thicker. Then more water goes from the blood into the urine. This water washes out other things, too. Vitamins and minerals, proteins and fats are lost along with the sugar and water.

That's why the warning signs develop. If you have diabetes, your kidneys have to make a lot of urine because they are getting rid of the extra sugar from the blood. So you may have to urinate a lot. You are also thirsty all the time because you are losing so much water. You feel unusually weak and tired because your body can't use sugar for the energy it needs to function properly. You are hungry because you are losing so many good food materials, which are getting washed out in your urine.

Too much sugar in the blood can also cause more serious problems. People with diabetes have a high risk of getting heart disease. High blood sugar levels may cause eye problems, possibly even resulting in blindness. Poorly controlled diabetes may also cause dental problems, high blood pressure, kidney damage, and nerve damage, which may produce pain and

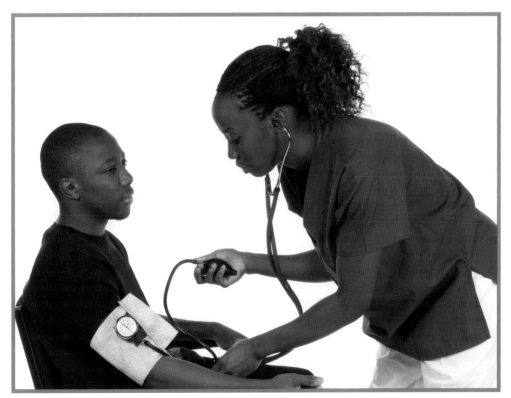

Poorly controlled diabetes can cause high blood pressure and other serious health problems.

numbness. Cuts and other wounds of diabetes patients are more likely to get infected than those in people without diabetes, and they do not heal as quickly. Many people with diabetes have problems with their feet, where even small cuts become more serious. In severe cases, part of the foot may have to be amputated (removed).

What's in a Name?

The name *diabetes* comes from a Greek word meaning "a siphon," a U-shaped tube that transfers liquid from one container to another. Ancient Greek physicians noticed that when people with diabetes drank large amounts of liquid, the fluid seemed to run right through them, as water runs through a siphon, and they would have to urinate often.

4

WHAT CAUSES DIABETES?

More than 18 million Americans have diabetes. Most of these people are adults, but health experts say that more children are getting diabetes than ever before. This may be because many kids today are eating too much food that is high in fat and sugar. They are also not getting enough exercise. This lack of exercise may lead to obesity—being extremely overweight. The extra weight is stored as body fat, which can lead to insulin resistance, a condition in which body cells are unable to use insulin effectively. Gaining a lot of weight increases a person's chance for developing type 2 diabetes. There is no link between obesity and type 1 diabetes.

Researchers believe that an overweight person is more likely to develop diabetes if someone in his or her

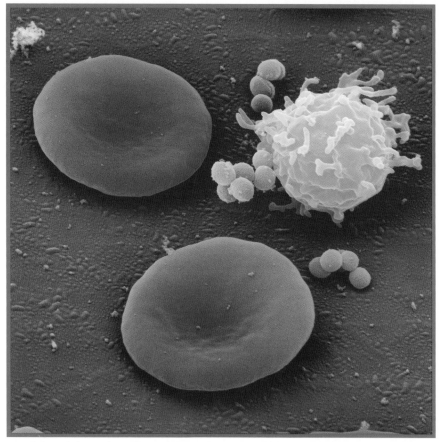

A white blood cell (white) is attacking bacteria (yellow).

family has it. Studies have shown that diabetes can be inherited when genes are passed down from one generation to another. Certain genes may play an important role in the development of diabetes. But even if someone in your family does have the disease, that doesn't mean you will get it.

Researchers have found that type 1 diabetes may be caused by infection with some viruses (tiny disease germs), such as those that cause the common cold or mumps. When you get sick, your body normally does a good job of defending itself. Germs are quickly spotted by special defending cells and these cells fight off the germs. But the body's defenders may make a mistake and attack islet cells, too. Insulin-producing cells are damaged, and the pancreas can no longer produce enough insulin to keep the blood sugar level under control. This can lead to type 1 diabetes.

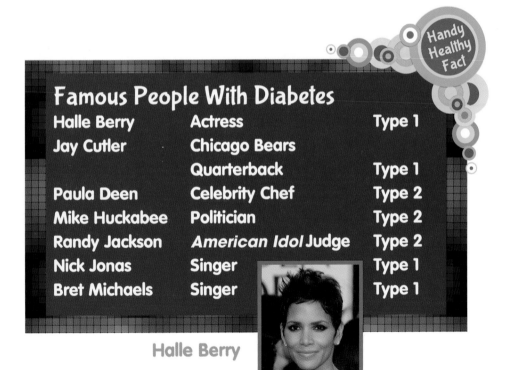

Handy Healthy Fact

Famous People With Diabetes

Halle Berry	Actress	Type 1
Jay Cutler	Chicago Bears Quarterback	Type 1
Paula Deen	Celebrity Chef	Type 2
Mike Huckabee	Politician	Type 2
Randy Jackson	*American Idol* Judge	Type 2
Nick Jonas	Singer	Type 1
Bret Michaels	Singer	Type 1

Halle Berry

Activity 1: Diabetes Definitions

Find out how well you understand diabetes. Choose the best definition for each word. (Do not write in this book! Instead write your answers on a piece of paper and check them against the answers below.)

1. Islets
2. Pancreas
3. Type 2 diabetes
4. Glucose
5. Starch
6. Insulin
7. Glucagon
8. Type 1 diabetes
9. Obesity
10. Glucose monitor

A. Hormone that lowers blood sugar level
B. Complex carbohydrate
C. Affects mainly children
D. High risk of developing type 2 diabetes
E. Hormone that raises blood sugar level
F. Hormone-producing cells in the pancreas
G. Simple sugar
H. Tests blood sugar level
I. Produces insulin and glucagon
J. Affects mainly adults over the age of forty

Answer Key: 1. F; 2. I; 3. J; 4. G; 5. B; 6. A; 7. E; 8. C; 9. D; 10. H.

22

5

TESTING FOR DIABETES

The medical name for diabetes is diabetes mellitus. Mellitus means "honey." It is used in the name because sugar that passes out into the urine gives it a sweet taste. Years ago, doctors would actually make a diagnosis by tasting a patient's urine! Later, doctors had tests and machines that could do the "tasting" for them.

Doctors no longer use urine tests to detect diabetes. Now they depend more on blood tests. Urine tests do a poor job of showing your blood glucose level.

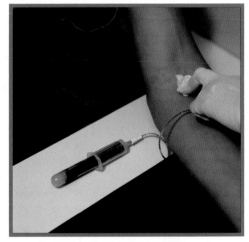

A doctor or nurse will take some blood from your arm to test for diabetes.

Glucose doesn't "spill over" into the urine until there is already quite a lot of glucose in the blood.

If you have symptoms that suggest diabetes, you should see a doctor right away. The easiest way for the doctor to detect diabetes is to do a plasma glucose test. This test measures how much glucose is in the blood.

Handy Healthy Fact

Super Sniffers

Everybody knows about Seeing Eye dogs that help blind people. But did you know there are dogs specially trained to sniff out diabetes? It's true! Dogs are super sniffers. Their sense of smell is 10,000 times better than that of a human. When a person's blood sugar level becomes too low or too high, the body gives off a certain odor. A fully trained dog can sniff out these changes in the blood. Then the dog alerts the owner by barking, whining, licking a hand, or some other signal. The dog can actually pick up a problem with the person's blood sugar level 20 minutes before a blood test can detect it—that's before any symptoms show up.

Blood can be taken through a needle in your arm or even with a little finger prick. Only a small amount of blood is needed.

Although a glucose test can be done any time of the day, the results will vary greatly depending on when you last ate. (Remember, eating raises the blood sugar level.) A fasting plasma glucose test is a better way to test for diabetes. This test is taken in the morning, before you have eaten anything. Normally after fasting, a person's blood contains less than 100 milligrams of glucose in each deciliter of blood. But a person with diabetes will have a fasting glucose level that is more than 126 mg/dl. Two fasting glucose tests taken on different days are needed to make a diagnosis of diabetes.

The glucose tolerance test gives more information on how the body handles sugar. The blood sugar is first tested after fasting. Then a patient drinks a concentrated sugar solution. Blood samples are taken several times over the next three hours and tested for the amount of glucose. At first the glucose drink makes the blood sugar level rise, but then the level falls. It is usually back to normal after two or three hours. In people with diabetes, the blood sugar rises much higher after

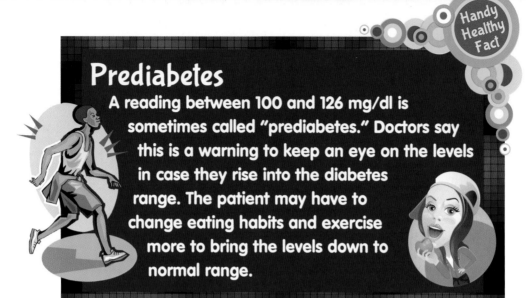

Prediabetes

A reading between 100 and 126 mg/dl is sometimes called "prediabetes." Doctors say this is a warning to keep an eye on the levels in case they rise into the diabetes range. The patient may have to change eating habits and exercise more to bring the levels down to normal range.

taking the glucose drink, and it falls more slowly. Even after three hours it may still be high.

Once diabetes is diagnosed, treatment should begin right away. As you know, high glucose levels can lead to serious problems.

6

TREATING DIABETES

Because diabetes is caused by a lack of working insulin, it makes sense that a common treatment is to put this hormone into the body. Unfortunately, there is no insulin pill or liquid you can drink. Instead, insulin must be injected. The needle doesn't squirt insulin directly into the blood. Instead, it goes into a muscle or fatty area. That way, the body can absorb the hormone more slowly rather than all at once. Some common places for injecting insulin are the thighs, buttocks, belly, or upper arms.

This person is giving herself an insulin injection.

Why Does Insulin Have to Be Injected?

No one likes getting shots, but people with diabetes have to have them every single day. Insulin must be injected. It would never work if it were in pill form. After being swallowed, the insulin would be destroyed by the stomach's digestive juices.

People with type 1 diabetes who do not make any insulin need daily insulin shots to keep their condition under control. But most people can't go to the doctor every single day for shots. That's why there are special kits that allow diabetes patients to give insulin shots in their own homes. Parents or other responsible adults usually give insulin shots to their young children with diabetes, but older kids can learn to give insulin shots to themselves. Teens with diabetes say that at first, it can be a little scary giving

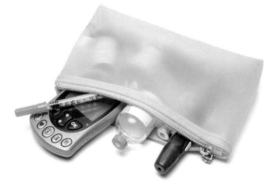

Diabetics use special kits that have all the tools they need to give themselves insulin shots.

yourself a shot, but after a while it becomes a routine like getting dressed or brushing your teeth.

There are some devices that make taking insulin easier. An automatic injector can shoot the needle into your skin, so that you hardly feel it. It's quick and easy. Insulin pens are a popular choice, too. An insulin pen looks just like a regular pen, but instead of a writing tip, it has a needle. And instead of an ink cartridge, it contains an insulin cartridge. Insulin pens are easy to use and can be carried around in a pocket. Jet injectors give insulin without even using a needle. The insulin is shot out so fast that it goes right into the skin.

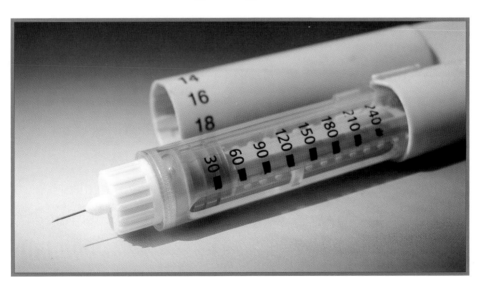

An insulin pen is another way of injecting insulin into the body.

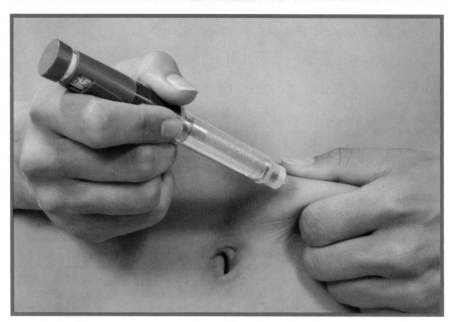

It is best to get an insulin shot before a meal.

Insulin shots need to be given several times every day, the way insulin is released from a healthy pancreas. Normally, a person's body produces insulin in response to food, which boosts the blood glucose levels. As the blood glucose levels fall between meals, so does the insulin production. To keep blood glucose levels normal, people with diabetes should receive insulin three times a day (before each meal) and another one at night before bed.

Several different kinds of insulin help to control the blood glucose level. Short-acting insulin works quickly and is good for taking before a meal. Long- or medium-acting insulin takes longer to start working but lasts longer. The nighttime injection keeps the glucose level normal during sleep.

Many people who have type 2 diabetes don't need daily insulin injections. They may take pills to keep their blood sugar under control. The pills do not contain insulin. They contain a drug that helps the body make more insulin or use insulin more effectively.

Exercise and diet are also important in keeping the diabetes under control. You burn sugar for energy when you exercise, and the blood glucose level decreases. Exercise also burns up food that might otherwise be stored in the body as fat. It helps to avoid obesity, which can make diabetes symptoms worse.

What about diet? You might think that someone with diabetes should never eat sugar or any sweet foods. Actually, though, it is more complicated than that. Everybody needs *some* sugar, but the body can get it from starches and other foods. The problem with eating candy or other high-sugar foods is that much of their sugar doesn't need to be digested. It goes right into the blood, and the blood glucose level shoots up. Then you

Insulin Pump

Having to inject yourself several times a day may seem like a hassle. So how would you like a device that does it for you automatically? An insulin pump is about the size of a cell phone and can clip onto your belt or be carried in your pocket. It is attached to a flexible plastic tube and a needle that is inserted under the skin and taped in place. A tiny built-in computer operates a pump that sends exactly the right amount of insulin into your body. You can also deliver an extra dose just before a meal. You have to do some experimenting first to figure out the right amount of insulin flow.

Researchers are working on "artificial pancreas" devices that are even more automatic. They combine a pump with a monitor to test the amount of glucose in the blood. A tiny computer predicts how the blood sugar level will change over the next 24 hours, depending on what the person eats. It adjusts the insulin dose automatically—just like a real pancreas.

need more insulin—fast! Starches and other complex carbohydrates, such as those found in bread, pasta, or rice, do need to be digested. So they send glucose into the blood slowly and gradually.

Some people with type 2 diabetes do have to take insulin if other treatments are not enough to control the condition.

Some patients with type 1 diabetes have received pancreas transplants. Part or all of a healthy pancreas is placed in a patient. People with successful pancreas transplants may not need to take insulin anymore and may have normal blood glucose levels. The problem with getting a transplant, however, is that the body may attack the new pancreas. The transplanted organ may even shrivel up and die. Doctors call this rejection of the transplant. Patients need to take special drugs to make

Pasta is a complex carbohydrate that delivers glucose to the body slowly.

Activity 2: Sugar vs. Starch

Making models of sugars and starches can help you understand how foods are used for energy. You need construction paper, scissors, and tape. Cut out fifteen strips of paper, each measuring an inch (about 2.5 cm) wide. Curve one strip into a loop and tape the ends together. This is like a glucose molecule. It is a simple sugar. Now make two more strips into loops, but before you tape the second one together, link it with the first. This is like a sucrose (table sugar) molecule, which is made of two simple sugars, linked together. Now take all the rest of the strips you cut out, and make them into a chain. This is like a starch molecule (but real starch has thousands of links).

Only simple sugars can be used directly for energy. Sucrose and starches have to be broken down into simple sugars to supply energy. Unpeel the tape on a link of the sucrose molecule and pull it out of the other link. This is like what the body has to do to get energy from sucrose. Now take one link at a time off the "starch" chain. Imagine how long it would take for a real starch molecule! That is why complex carbohydrates (such as starches) provide energy at a much slower rate.

sure this does not happen. But antirejection drugs can have some bad side effects.

Researchers have turned to the idea of transplanting only the islet cells, rather than the whole pancreas. Remember, islet cells produce insulin. Scientists believe that transplanting islet cells is less dangerous than transplanting the whole pancreas. But they still don't know how many islet cells are needed and exactly where they should be transplanted. And patients must take special drugs to prevent the body from rejecting the islet cells.

7

LIVING WITH DIABETES

There is no cure for diabetes at this time. It is a condition a person has to live with every single day. But diabetes can be controlled, and people who have it can live long, healthy lives.

A health care specialist can help patients come up with a good plan that is just right for that individual. What may be good for one person may not be good for another. For example, the amount of insulin needs to be adjusted according to each person's individual needs.

Monitoring glucose is an important part of living with diabetes. People with diabetes need to check their blood glucose levels several times a day to see how well their condition is being controlled. This helps to give a better idea of how much insulin is needed.

Some people get involved. They may raise money and awareness of the disease. This group is walking to help the JDRF (Juvenile Diabetes Research Foundation).

Blood glucose monitors are devices that can measure blood sugar levels in a matter of minutes. Using a monitor regularly helps you figure out how much insulin you need.

Blood sugar is tested by pricking a finger or earlobe and placing a drop of blood into a small portable machine that provides a digital readout of blood sugar levels. Glucose monitoring is very important because it helps to avoid serious problems that may develop.

Home glucose monitoring devices make checking blood sugar easy.

When too much sugar is in the blood, that means that glucose is not getting into the body cells. So the cells can't use the sugar for energy, and they have to use something else, such as protein or fats. Taking protein out of the muscles makes them weak. When fats are burned, they give a lot of energy, but they also form chemicals called ketones. Too many ketones can poison cells and make a person really sick. People can check for ketones with special urine test strips. Ketones in the urine are usually a sign that more insulin is needed to keep the blood sugar under control. A doctor or nurse can advise what to do.

"Ouchless" Monitors

Many people—especially kids—don't like pricking their fingers several times every day. So researchers have been trying to create glucose monitors that don't need to prick the skin at all. The GlucoWatch G2 Biographer, worn on the wrist, uses a tiny electric current to draw fluid through the skin into a pad, where glucose is measured. The amount of electricity is too small to hurt or even tingle. This GlucoWatch also has a built-in alarm to warn the person when the glucose level is too high or too low.

Missing doses of insulin, eating too much, or getting an infection or injury may lead to a serious condition called diabetic coma. Headaches, tiredness, confusion, stomach pain, and breathing problems may develop as ketones from fats build up. The person may even pass out. Quick emergency care is needed to diagnose and treat the problem.

Sometimes people with diabetes take too much insulin by mistake, causing a low blood sugar level.

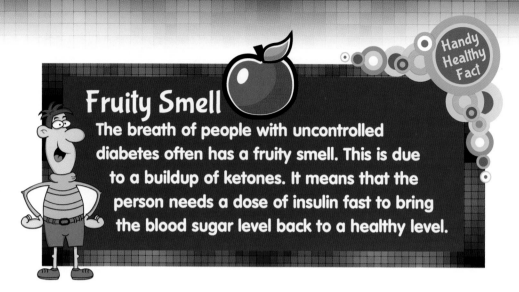

Fruity Smell

The breath of people with uncontrolled diabetes often has a fruity smell. This is due to a buildup of ketones. It means that the person needs a dose of insulin fast to bring the blood sugar level back to a healthy level.

This can be dangerous. Too much glucose will go out of the blood, and not enough will go to the brain. The brain needs a lot of energy, and without enough glucose it won't work properly. If the blood glucose level falls too low, insulin shock may result. The person may feel chilly, sweaty, hungry, nervous, and irritable and may faint. Insulin shock is a dangerous condition that needs immediate emergency care.

Sometimes, such as when you skip a meal, you can have a bad reaction even if you take the right amount of insulin. When you don't eat at the usual time, your blood sugar level drops. But if you have diabetes, you may already have taken your scheduled insulin shot. The insulin was supposed to lower your blood sugar to normal after a meal. But if you don't eat, there will be no extra glucose in your blood. Instead, insulin will take away some of the sugar your brain needs.

Exercise burns up glucose, so exercising more than usual can also cause the blood sugar level to fall very low. Eating snacks between meals and before exercising can help you avoid an insulin reaction.

Many people with diabetes carry around a quick fix to correct low blood sugar. If they feel dizzy and sick and think they might be getting an insulin reaction, they have hard candy or a sweet drink, such as orange juice or soda. The sugar goes right into the blood and brings the level back to normal. Students with diabetes should talk to their teacher about bringing snacks to class so they can avoid any blood sugar level problems.

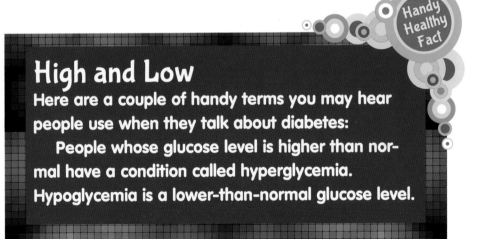

Handy Healthy Fact

High and Low
Here are a couple of handy terms you may hear people use when they talk about diabetes:
People whose glucose level is higher than normal have a condition called hyperglycemia. Hypoglycemia is a lower-than-normal glucose level.

It's a good idea to wear a medical identification bracelet or necklace and to carry an I.D. card in case of an emergency. Information on your illness and what to do in case of an insulin reaction, as well as your name and the name and number of someone to contact, can save your life.

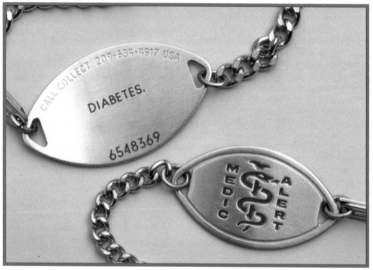

A medical identification bracelet alerts doctors that you have diabetes in case you are too sick to tell them.

GLOSSARY

blood sugar level—The amount of glucose in the blood.

carbohydrates—Starches and sugars, the body's main energy sources.

diabetes—A condition in which insulin is not produced or does not properly control the body's use and storage of sugar, resulting in abnormally high amounts of glucose in the blood; extra glucose may also spill over into the urine.

diabetic coma—A serious condition due to a lack of enough insulin, causing a buildup of ketones from using fats for energy.

diagnosis—Identifying a condition from its signs and symptoms.

digestion—The process by which food is broken down into smaller parts that the body can use.

fasting plasma glucose test—A diagnostic test in which the blood glucose level is measured. It has to be taken early in the morning before eating.

genes—Chemicals inside each cell that carry inherited traits.

glucagon—A hormone that raises the amount of sugar in the blood.

glucose—The most common kind of sugar in the blood. The body uses glucose for energy.

glucose tolerance test—A test for diabetes in which a person drinks a glucose solution after fasting and the blood sugar is measured several times over the next three hours.

hormone—A chemical that helps to control the body's activities.

hyperglycemia—A higher-than-normal blood sugar level.

hypoglycemia—A lower-than-normal blood sugar level.

inherited—Passed on by genes from parents to children.

injected—Sent into the body through a hollow needle.

insulin—A hormone that controls the level of sugar in the blood.

insulin resistance—A condition in which the cells are unable to use insulin effectively.

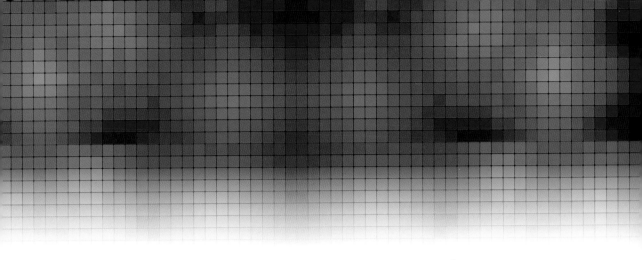

insulin shock—A dangerous reaction to too much insulin in the blood.

islets (pronounced EYE-lets)—Clusters of insulin-producing cells scattered throughout the pancreas.

ketones—Chemicals that are formed when the body burns fats for energy.

obesity—The condition of being extremely overweight.

pancreas—An organ that produces hormones, such as insulin and glucagon, which help to control the amount of glucose in the blood; it also makes digestive juices, which help to break down food.

plasma glucose test—A diagnostic test in which the blood glucose level is measured; it can be taken at any time of the day.

secrete—To release, or send out.

starch—A food substance found in bread, potatoes, and pasta that the body breaks down into sugars.

urinate—To pass liquid body wastes (urine) produced by the kidneys.

LEARN MORE

Books

American Diabetes Association. *What to Expect When You Have Diabetes: 170 Tips For Living Well with Diabetes.* Intercourse, Pa.: Good Books, 2008.

Brill, Marlene Targ. *Diabetes.* Minneapolis, Minn.: Twenty-First Century Books, 2012.

Ehrman, M. K. *Living with Diabetes.* Minneapolis, Minn.: ABDO Pub., 2012.

Hood, Korey K. *Type 1 Teens: A Guide to Managing Your Life with Diabetes.* Washington, D.C.: Magination Press: American Psychological Association, 2010.

Klosterman, Lorrie. *Endocrine System.* New York: Marshall Cavendish Benchmark, 2009.

Web Sites

American Diabetes Association. *Living With Diabetes.*
    <http://www.diabetes.org/living-with-diabetes/
    parents-and-kids/>

Juvenile Diabetes Research Foundation International.
    JDRF Kids Online.
    <http://kids.jdrf.org/>

INDEX